Northern Narratives #1

TALL TALES OF ALASKA THE RED DOG SALOON

Tales from the Gold Rush & More

W.R. Kozey

ISBN 978-1-954896-38-3 paperback
ISBN 978-1-954896-40-6 ebook
ISBN 978-1-954896-41-3 audio
Cover photograph and illustrations, Sam Grubitz
Red Dog photograph and logo, Red Dog Saloon

Printed in United States of America

Fathom Publishing Company
PO Box 200448 | Anchorage, AK 99520
Fathom Publishing.com

To Eric and Tracy Forst
for their unwavering dedication
to the Saloon and their continued
commitment to creating
a great atmosphere at the Red Dog
for tourists and employees alike.

Contents

Acknowledgments

I would like to begin by acknowledging the Indigenous peoples of Alaska and their ancestral homelands. I want to pay my respects to all the Tribes that call this land their home and recognize the deep and abiding connections they have to this place.

I would also like to acknowledge the brave and tenacious souls who traveled north to Alaska during the gold rush seeking fortune and adventure. For it is their experiences and struggles that line these pages and without them there is no book.

Finally, I want to express my gratitude to all those who have contributed to this work, whether through guidance, support, or inspiration. This collection would not have been possible without their contributions—thank you.

How old is the Red Dog Saloon?

When Alaska was a territory, the bars and saloons were not required to have the business licenses nor the liquor licenses that are needed today; therefore, the origin story of the Red Dog Saloon in Juneau, Alaska, is not widely documented. However, locals know it was established in the late nineteenth century and has been a popular gathering place for gold miners, sailors, and other patrons ever since.

As the story goes, the saloon opened its doors—or flaps—as a tent on Douglas Island, just across the Gastineau Channel from Juneau. They chose this location because Douglas was home to one of the most lucrative gold mines of its time, the Treadwell Mine. And, before they built the bridge connecting the Island to the city of Juneau, if those miners were ever thirsty for a drink or longing for the company of one of those fine ladies of the night, they needed to ferry into town to go the bars and brothel. Well, the original saloon owner saw this as an opportunity and brought the beer and, consequently, the ladies, directly to his clientele over on Douglas.

The Red Dog Saloon was born. And for a while, business was great; however during World War II, many of the gentlemen working the mines, docks, and fishing boats left town, either going overseas to fight or down south to work in the factories. The Red Dog had lost its customer base, and if the saloon was to survive, the owner needed to do something quick.

So, the saloon was moved from the island into the city. Initially, the building stood in Juneau's red-light district on the west side of South Franklin Street, right across from the Alaskan Hotel. In this new location, the saloon's clientele changed, and it became known for its rough and rowdy atmosphere, with gambling, drinking, and brawls being common occurrences. And, according to local lore, it was during one of these more unsavory nights that somebody "accidentally" started a fire.

Now, there are a number of different theories for how the fire started. Some say it was an old kerosene lamp that got knocked over; others say it was a cigar that got tossed into the sawdust; hell, some even say it wasn't anyone at all, and the saloon's old, faulty wiring was to blame. One thing is for certain though, the building went up faster than a box of matchsticks and the saloon burnt down in 1967.

Thankfully, the saloon didn't lose everything that night and the owner was able to salvage about seventy percent of the saloon's adornments. That means, when it reopened on the east side of South Franklin Street, now right beside the Alaskan Hotel, the saloon had that same wild-west flavor that people had grown to love.

That said, it wasn't there long though, because in 1972 the bar changed hands, and its new owner had a different vision for his newly acquired saloon. He'd taken notice of the slow rise in steamship traffic over the years and the steady increase of travelers lining Juneau's streets in the summers and he wanted to be part of the action. To do that, he needed to be closer to the water, so in 1986 the new owner commissioned the construction of the building the saloon now resides in. And, in 1987 the saloon moved to its current location.

Now, with all that moving and all those tourists later, you may very well be thinking that the saloon's authenticity could be called into question. Well, you'd be wrong. The Red Dog Saloon Preservation Group watched over every piece and every parcel that made its way to 278 South Franklin.

That's right, an entire committee of people in town saw to it that the Red Dog Saloon stayed intact, just the way it was. And they didn't just do it for themselves, they did it for you too.

So, when you find yourself coming back through those swingin' doors again, looking for another round, take a moment and take in some of that history. All of the wood paneling on the walls is from the original saloon. They used the salvaged lumber from the old building to construct the upstairs seating area. Most of the critters like the moose, halibut, and Kodiak grizzly bear are originals. And so too, is some of the memorabilia like, the state seal of Alaska, the forty-nine-star American flag, and of course, Wyatt Earp's pistol.

Was the saloon ever a brothel?

As we learned in our last story, with miners comes beer. But that is not all that typically follows men and money to the far reaches of the world. No, where there is wealth, there will always be women. And, during the gold rush, plenty of those women found themselves in Alaska, keeping many a miner company on those long Alaskan nights.

That being said, the answer to your question is no. Contrary to the pretty little outfits the waitresses wear at the Red Dog, the saloon was never a brothel. In Juneau, during the late 1800s and early 1900s, this type of business generally transpired at the Alaskan Hotel. Men from all walks of life would come to the hotel to indulge in their more carnal desires. And the madam, a woman named Black Mary, well, she was a savvy businesswoman who knew exactly how to run a tight ship—her ladies of the night were well kept and well trained and the johns always left satisfied.

However, with great success comes great risk. The law enforcement in town were always looking for ways to shut down Black Mary, and her thriving enterprise. They would raid the hotel on a regular basis, trying their best to catch the ladies in the act, but somehow Black Mary and her girls always managed to escape.

Now, many have their theories for how the women got away with it all.

Some say it was as simple as bribing the officers, while others say Black Mary had an inside man or woman, one that would inform her when the police planned to perform their raids. But if you ask any of the bartenders in town, one rumor will continuously come up, and that is the theory of the underground tunnel.

There is no physical evidence of a tunnel, nor does it make any sense to build such an elaborate shaft, but it is said that there used to be a tunnel running from the basement of the Alaskan Hotel all the way to Douglas Island, across the narrow gap of the Gastineau Channel.

As the story goes, the tunnel was built during the gold rush by a group of laborers using only their pickaxes and shovels to dig through the rocky terrain. Black Mary had hired them for this specific task to provide herself, and her ladies, a sure-fire way to escape.

And it worked. When Juneau's law enforcement would break down the door of the hotel, Black Mary and her girls would flee through the tunnel to safety. When they emerged on Douglas Island, the women and the johns would simply blend in with the Treadwell miners and their wives and disappear.

This legend has persisted for decades, even after the brothel stopped running and the hotel became exactly that, a hotel. Even now, people still whisper about it, wondering if it was real or just a myth. Some even claim to have seen the entrance to the tunnel with their own eyes, hidden somewhere in the basement of the hotel bar. Sadly, we won't know, not until years from now when the Alaskan Hotel is torn down or turned into a museum and the rumors are finally put to rest. Until then, we will just have to remember a time long gone when the wilds of Alaska were still untamed and anything was possible.

How did the Red Dog Saloon get its name?

After learning about how old the bar is and the fact that it wasn't the brothel in town, your next question is sure to be about how the saloon got its name. And no, despite what most people think, the bar isn't named after the little red Scottie on its logo. As a matter-a-fact, the Red Dog's red dog wasn't even always a Scottie. First it was a Husky, then a Dachshund, and only more recently has the Scottie appeared as the puppy of choice. So no, the bar isn't named after a lovable red puppy. Instead, to find the origin story of the world-famous Red Dog Saloon's name, we need go back, back to the beginnings of the Alaskan gold rush.

As you read in a previous story, back when the Treadwell Mine was at its peak and Juneau was a bustling gold-mining town, the original saloon got its start selling beer out of a tent right beside the mine on Douglas Island. And the saloon was highly successful, quickly becoming a favorite spot for the mining community to come and unwind, share stories, and raise a glass to their hard-earned successes.

This was a great time for the saloon, but the little establishment was growing in popularity, and it still didn't have a name. The owner threw around a few ideas but none ended up sticking.

What did stick, though, was the reddish-brown clay pulled out of the mines that coated all of the miners' clothes. The clay ended up on everything: the glasses, the chairs, the tables, and even the tent itself. It stuck so much so that eventually, the slang term the miners used to describe the clay became synonymous with the saloon itself, and the tent became known as the Redawg Saloon.

Well, as the gold began to dry up and the miners left in droves to find work elsewhere, the saloon was in danger of going out of business. The Redawg owner needed to either make a change or close up shop. So, the saloon ditched the tent and moved into town, opening up in the building across the street from Juneau's brothel—the Alaskan Hotel.

The bar owner wanted to stay true to the saloon's roots; so, to preserve the memory of the tent on Douglas and the town's rich gold-mining history, he dedicated the saloon's interior to the gold-mining industry. He collected artifacts, memorabilia, and relics of the wild west to display all over his walls.

And as more and more travelers came to Juneau, word spread about the saloon and its storied history. And soon, the saloon became a hub of activity once again; only this time, it was filled with tourists.

This was great for the owner, but he then had another problem—those tourists wanted to bring home souvenirs to their friends and family to commemorate their time in Juneau, and their time at the Redawg Saloon. Now, of course, at first, this doesn't sound like a problem at all. But if you think about it, who wants to buy a T-shirt with a picture of a big ol' lump of red clay on it?

Thankfully, it didn't take much imagination to change it—the saloon owner split the name down the middle, adopted a pretty red puppy as the bar's mascot, and started slapping pictures of it on just about anything he could find.

Years have passed since the change and, now, the long-established Red Dog Saloon is the most popular man-made tourist destination in Alaska. People from all over the world come to visit and get a glimpse into the past.

And so, the legacy of the saloon and its connection to Juneau's gold mines lives on, regardless of whether or not its patrons recognize its ties to the reddish-brown tailings that were once pulled from the Treadwell Mine—the same tailings that make up the reclaimed ground underneath Juneau's boardwalks and the fill used for the area on which the Red Dog now resides.

What is the deal with the dollar bills?

I'm sure you're getting tired of hearing what I'm about to tell you, but like so many other answers to your questions in this collection, the dollar bills hung up at not only the Red Dog Saloon, but at plenty of other bars across Alaska too, have their origins in the gold rush.

Now, what you mostly hear about the Alaskan gold rush, and even what you've read in this book up until now, is that in the late 1800s, thousands of people from all over the world flocked to the state, eager to make their fortunes in the rough wilderness of Alaska.

But what you won't hear about, is how challenging these trips up north actually were during this time. The prospectors of the past didn't have the planes, trains, or cruise liners that we have today. Not to mention, the travelers were often ill-prepared for the harsh conditions, rough seas, and constant storms of the Pacific Northwest. Because of this, many suffered from exposure and malnutrition along the journey, and if they didn't have access to proper medical supplies, oftentimes, they didn't make it.

People made this trip anyway though, mainly because they thought the going would get easier once they made it to Alaska. Only it wasn't. To reach the gold fields, those who survived the seas now had to traverse hundreds of miles of rugged wilderness including mountains and glaciers. In addition to the hike, many miners had to contend with harsh weather—including sub-zero temperatures, high winds, and heavy snowfall, which made it difficult to work and travel.

Now, most of you reading this story probably knew the trip to Alaska couldn't have been easy in the 1800s already, so I'm beating a dead horse. But, what you have yet to learn about this journey is that it was extremely expensive. Most of the miners spent their entire life's fortune just to get to Alaska with no guarantees of finding any gold.

So, what started happening in Juneau, the gateway to the goldrush, was that once the miners had purchased their provisions in town, they'd head to one of the local taverns or saloons to have a drink before going prospecting. Afterward, before heading out, they'd take one of their last dollar bills, sign it, and hand it over to the bartender. The bartender would then take the dollar bill and staple it behind the bar for safekeeping. This way, when the miners returned from prospecting—sometimes weeks, even months later—and they hadn't struck it rich or found any gold, at least they knew they'd have a dollar bill waiting for them at the saloon to buy a beer or whiskey when they got back.

To this day, bars in Alaska continue to hang dollar bills on their walls as a symbol of this history and a tribute to those who took the risk and braved the treacherous journey north. The only difference is that now, the bartenders just take your money. So, don't be expecting your dollar bill to be waiting for you when you find yourself back at the Red Dog Saloon for another round!

Why is there sawdust on the floor?

There are several great reasons for why the bars in the harsh and rugged state of Alaska carpet their floors with sawdust. For starters, during the gold rush, these bars survived mainly on serving drinks and food to tired and cold gold miners. These miners would come into the bars covered in mud and snow from their long days of searching for gold in the icy tundra. And thankfully, the sawdust absorbed the moisture and mud from the miner's boots, kept the floors clean, and made it easy to remove the messes when they got to be too much.

Another good reason for spreading sawdust in a bar full of miners is to reduce the noise and prevent accidents. Miners are known to be a rowdy crowd and often stumble after having too much to drink. The sawdust helps swallow the sound of their footsteps and helps soften their landings when they fall off of their stools.

Additionally, spreading sawdust in Alaskan bars helped mask the unpleasant odors and spills. Miners often came into the bar straight from work covered in sweat and dust. The sawdust added a pleasant, woodsy fragrance to the bar which helped cover up any unpleasant odors and absorb any spills, keeping the bar smelling fresh, instead of stinky miners.

Now, these are all reasonable explanations as to why saloons all across Alaska, including the Red Dog Saloon, cover their floors with sawdust; however, the real reason why they did it in the beginning was slightly more nefarious.

Like many of the bars in Juneau, the majority of the Red Dog's patrons were miners when the saloon opened up. And, these miners would go out to the bars and brothel after a long day's work looking to spend what little gold nuggets and what few silver dollars they had on a good time. This was not a secret, nor was it the reason for the sawdust. No, the real reason has to do with what would happen to those gold nuggets and those silver dollars once their owners had had a few drinks—they had a nasty habit of falling out of their owner's pockets.

Yes, hardwood floors made it easy to sweep and mop, but it also made it easy for the miners—drunk or not—to find the gold or silver that had fallen. Thankfully, several other bars in the Klondike were already using sawdust to prevent noise, odor, and accidents, so nobody thought twice when the Red Dog Saloon opened its doors with a fresh coat of the stuff on its floor. What people didn't know, though, was that every night, after all the miners had gone home, the saloon would rake up the dust to collect what gold and silver had been dropped.

Now, from my understanding, the practice was very lucrative for the owner and whatever bartender was working, oftentimes making more off of what had fallen to the floor than what was sold at the bar. Unfortunately, the bartenders now will never know because the current owners of the saloon are not nearly as nefarious. They try their best to return everything they find in the dust to its rightful owner, and the continuation of using sawdust is solely for the purpose of giving travelers from far and wide a glimpse into the gold rush days.

That said, be wary; the sawdust has a mind of its own and is still just as likely to rob you of your riches if you're not careful!

What is in a Duck Fart?
(Was the Duck Fart invented at the Red Dog Saloon?)

Similar to many other stories in this book, the detailed history of the "Duck Fart" shot sold at the Red Dog Saloon in Alaska is unknown. But one thing is certain: this unique, Alaskan-created cocktail made from three ingredients—coffee liquor, Irish cream, and Canadian whiskey—is famous worldwide thanks to the saloon and its cruise ship passenger customer base.

Now, despite the drink clearly gaining its fame from the Red Dog, its origin story is only somewhat agreed upon. There are several theories of how it came to be created, but if you ask any of the local bartenders here in Juneau, they'll tell you that the drink originated at the Red Dog Saloon, just not the one in Juneau. The one they're talking about was located in Fairbanks, Alaska, until it closed down, but not before it being made famous by a little-known singer-songwriter named Johnny Horton.

For those who don't know, Fairbanks is just 140 miles from the arctic circle and can get dreadfully cold even in the springtime. And, as the story goes, it was, in fact, during one of these spring storms that the Duck Fart was invented.

The storm blew in quickly that evening and, having been more fixated on the entertainment and libations than the weather, when it came time to close down the bar, the patrons were all caught off guard when they realized that the snow had in fact barricaded them all in. It was okay, though. No one seemed to mind that the snow showed no signs of slowing because, well, everyone just kept on drinking.

The group started with the top shelf—the bourbon, the scotch, the American whiskey—but soon, the high-end alcohol began to run out, and they were forced to lower their standards.

Eventually, the gang had gone through everything except the last three bottles with any liquid: the coffee liquor, the Irish cream, and the Canadian whiskey.

Now, to conserve the liquor, the creative bartender decided to use all three liquors in one glass; and to dress them up, he poured just a little bit of each in each glass and, using a maraschino cherry, he layered them.

One of the men took the tiniest of sips from his glass and immediately spit it out.

"It's awful!" The man spat.

"It's alcohol," barked another, and downed the contents in his glass.

Expecting the same result, the bartender took cover. However, to his surprise, he received a smile instead of another round of spittle.

Seeing their friend's reaction, the others followed suit and slammed their glasses back.

"Another round!" they all declared.

Relieved the shot was a hit, the bartender continued pouring. And, as the storm wore on, the warm, comforting flavors kept the group in a good mood.

After the storm had passed, and the authorities had removed the snow in front of the doors, the group dispersed and the bartender expected to never pour the concoction again. Yet, repeatedly, patrons who'd been snowed in that night kept coming back to the bar and ordering the shot. Eventually, others started ordering it too, and it was at this time they decided it needed a name.

Over and over, patrons would give suggestions like “Snow Storm Shot,” “Snowbound Sipper,” and “Blizzard Blast,” but none of them felt right to the bartender. It wasn’t until a new customer stumbled into the bar and ordered the unnamed drink and was about to sip it when someone stopped him.

“Don’t sip it,” he warned.

“Why?”

“It’ll taste like a duck’s ass if you do!”

“That’s it!” said the bartender. “I know what I’m going to call the shot!”

And as the new customer downed the shot, the bartender pulled out a piece of paper and scribbled the recipe down. At the top of the page in big bold letters, he wrote “Duck Fart.” And it’s been called that ever since.

Is that a grizzly bear?

Most tourists come to the Red Dog to see the girls, listen to the music, and catch a glimpse of Wyatt Earp's pistol. But there is a large brown bear that hangs directly above the pistol that tends to garner its own kind of attention. The bear's fierce snarl and giant paws constantly draw questions from the customers like: "How big is the bear?" "Where is its other half?" "And is that a grizzly?"

Well, if you listen carefully to my story here, you might get your answers.

Now, most of you, the saloon's patronage, are from the lower forty-eight, so I can cut you some slack for assuming it's just a plain ol' grizzly bear behind the bar because, technically, you're right. It is a grizzly hanging behind the bar, just not an ordinary one. The bear that hangs behind the bar to protect Wyatt Earp's pistol is a Kodiak grizzly bear, native only to Alaska's Kodiak Island.

Kodiak grizzly bears, also known as Kodiak brown bears, are some of the biggest grizzly bears in the world. And, so I'm told, the one that hangs on the wall of the Red Dog Saloon was hung at the height of where it stood on its hind legs. Now, I've never taken a tape measure to it, but that would make this bear just about twelve feet tall in its heyday.

Of course, there are many theories for why these bears have evolved to be so big: some say it is the abundance of salmon—the bear's primary source of protein. Others think the isolation of Kodiak Island, and the resulting absence of smaller grizzlies to mate with is what allows for the pure, uninterrupted strain of these giant bears. Yes, both of these theories logically explain why the Kodiak grizzly grows to be so big. But they aren't the real reason.

As the story goes, during the last ice age, polar bears of northern Alaska roamed the frozen tundra in search of food. Because of the extreme cold, this search brought them as far south as the Gulf of Alaska. And due to the harsh icy conditions prevalent at the time, the water separating the island of Kodiak from the mainland was frozen over, allowing the polar bears to cross over quite easily.

Once on the island, it was only a short time before the polar bears came across a population of grizzly bears living there. The grizzlies were smaller and less adapted to the cold than the polar bears, but were fierce and territorial. Nature knew it even before the bears did, but this combination was perfect for the Alaskan wilderness.

The polar bears and grizzlies eventually began to mate, and these new Kodiak bears thrived on the island. The offspring of these mixed-species relationships had the dense fur and sharp claws of the polar bear and the agility and strength of the grizzlies. This combination of attributes quickly elevated the Kodiaks to the top of the food chain.

And today, travelers from far and wide travel to the island of Kodiak to try to catch a glimpse at these massive, fiercely territorial bears that can't be found anywhere else.

What does the plaque under the bear say?

In the previous story, I told you about the bear hanging behind the bar at the Red Dog Saloon and some of its history, but there is still one question left to answer: what the heck does the plaque underneath it say?

There is a silver plaque on the bear's wall mount with a small engraving. The engraving reads: "Donated to the S.S. *Kodiak* by the people of Kodiak, Alaska, home of the world's largest brown bear."

Of course, the statement is plain enough. The bear was given to a Navy ship, the S.S. *Kodiak*. But what the plaque doesn't tell you is why the vessel received such a reward, nor does it explain how it ended up at the Red Dog Saloon. And since you asked so nicely, I'm here to happily answer both of these questions.

So, according to the tale, the captain of the S.S. *Kodiak* was a native Juneauite. And following in his father's footsteps, the boy always wanted to be a man of the sea, destined to spend his life fishing and navigating the treacherous waters of the North Pacific.

However when the Cold War broke out, a sense of duty to serve and protect his country drew the would-be captain away from Alaska and his family. Given much of his life was spent on the water, the Navy was the most logical place for him. So, he enlisted and quickly rose through the ranks. And when the USSR started testing their nuclear weapons, it made perfect sense for him to assume the rank of commanding officer on a ship destined for America's northernmost coastline.

The ship was the S.S. *Kodiak*, a fully functional battleship that ferried supplies and troops to the most remote areas of Alaska during the war. And throughout the war, the *Kodiak* braved storms, treacherous icebergs, and covert missions along the Aleutian Islands, all while never failing to deliver its cargo.

After the war, the people of the northern islands wanted to show appreciation for the vessel's service and its captain's bravery. And to do so, they held a grand ceremony in Juneau, the state's capital, presenting the captain with a mounted Kodiak grizzly bear.

The bear was a majestic specimen, with fur, brown like chocolate and claws as long as knives, making it a truly fitting tribute to the captain and the S.S. *Kodiak.*

However, the captain was now faced with a problem. He lived on his ship and there was nowhere on the S.S. *Kodiak* to hang a bear this size. The boat was already crowded with cargo and crew, and the bear would take up far too much space. So, the captain made an executive decision to leave it with his favorite bar in town, a place called the Red Dog Saloon.

He reasoned that the Red Dog Saloon catered to locals and tourists alike making it a perfect place to display the Alaskan people's respect and appreciation for those who served their country. The saloon's owner was delighted when the captain asked permission to leave the bear at the bar and wasted little time hanging it in a prominent place.

And so, the Kodiak grizzly found a

new home mounted on the wall behind the bar at the Red Dog Saloon, where it continues to catch the eye of more than one patron. The tourists take photos of it and buy rounds of drinks in its honor. And the locals and bar staff still tell stories about the legendary captain from Juneau who gifted the bear to the bar.

As for the captain, years passed and he grew old. After he retired from the sea, he settled in a small cabin outside of Juneau. Many thought the captain would ask for the bear back but he never did. Instead, he visited the saloon periodically, always sitting at the bar directly across from his prize, often looking up at the mounted bear on the wall and smiling.

Is that a jackalope, a male porcupine . . . What the heck is that thing?

So, if you're reading this book, you've most likely ventured into the Red Dog Saloon. And if you've done that, you already know that when you walk into the saloon, you experience a bit of sensory overload. There is sawdust on the floors, animals hanging on the walls, and pretty girls in corsets running around serving food and cold beverages.

It's really a lot to take in.

There is one particular critter on display that, if you didn't sit at the far end of the bar, you might have missed. It is the horny beaver.

No, no, this is not a joke. The saloon didn't just shove horns into the head of a porcupine—or at least that's what I'm told.

From my understanding, the horny beaver was a rare and elusive creature once native to Juneau, Alaska. The beavers grew horns because, well, after a few long, dark, and lonely winters up here everything gets a little horny.

This famed animal was a nocturnal creature, only coming out at night to forage for food, build its dam, or find a lucky mate. It was also a solitary animal, often preferring to keep to itself, but every so often, on the weekends, around two or three in the morning, patrons would leave the bars of downtown Juneau and see the beavers stumbling up and down

Franklin Street, seeming to be looking for something.

Soon, word spread about the existence of this magical animal, and hunters started flocking to Juneau from far and wide to try capture one to bring back home. And, despite the horny beaver's elusive nature, the hunter's relentlessness in unearthing it eventually led to its extinction, never to be seen on the streets of Juneau again.

Years have passed, and the legend of the horny beaver has faded into memory, but for those who lived in Juneau during its time, the memory of this noble animal has not been forgotten.

I fondly remember the little furry creature. And, if I had it my way, I would still be going out on the weekends in search of this elusive animal. Unfortunately, my wife doesn't let me go hunting anymore.

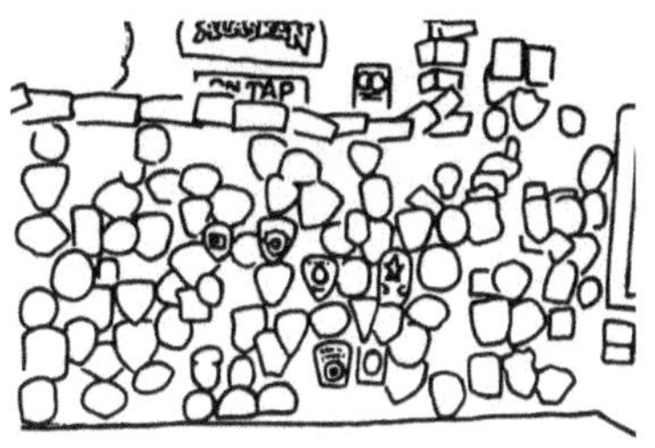

What is the story behind the police patches?

If you're asking this question, you can probably guess that this tradition has been going on for some time. This is because police, sheriffs, state troopers, and marshals have always been held in high regard in Alaska due to their efforts toward maintaining law and order throughout the state. This is especially true in gold-mining communities because these towns sprang up everywhere, often in remote areas.

Now, Juneau isn't as remote as some other places, but it is a gold-mining town which made it just as rowdy and chaotic as any of the others during the gold rush—and ripe for criminal activity.

Some common forms of criminal activity during the gold rush included theft and robbery. Miners and prospectors were often targeted by criminals who sought to steal hard-earned gold. There were also instances of fraud, where unscrupulous individuals would sell false mining claims or use other deceptive methods to exploit the gullible.

Moreover, gambling and prostitution were also common, as many miners and prospectors sought to blow off steam and enjoy themselves after a long day's work. This wasn't necessarily the problem, but these activities were often associated with violence and disorder, and the law enforcement officers were tasked with keeping the peace. And, lastly, in addition to these more routine crimes, there were occasional outbreaks of vigilante justice and clashes between rival mining claims. In these cases, law enforcement was instrumental in maintaining order and preventing these situations from escalating into full-blown conflict.

Now, I know what you're thinking. The saloon hung the badges as a bribe to get law enforcement to look the other way when these nefarious activities were happening under its roof. You wouldn't be wrong, but this was just an added bonus and not the real reason.

The Red Dog can proudly say that they hang badges as a way of showing respect to Alaska's rich law enforcement history.

And now that tradition carries on in the form of hanging first responder patches from all over the world.

Nevertheless, the first patch that was hung had more to do with location and logistics than anything else. When the Red Dog moved to its current location, the Juneau Police Department was housed right next door. And, for a time, the saloon became a bar frequented by mainly police officers and state troopers.

As the story goes, one evening the bar was full of officers looking to have a good time. And, one of the sergeants there that night thought it would be funny to perform a coin check—a fun game of comradery between servicemen, servicewomen, and law enforcement—where all must present a coin-sized item known as a challenge coin. The coin is often emblazoned with that individual's unit insignia, and if all of the officers in the room can present their challenge coins, the person initiating the coin check must buy a round. Conversely, if someone doesn't have their challenge coin, it is them that now must buy the round for everyone.

This may seem innocent enough, but what you need to know is that, in the past, it was considered a great dishonor to the unit if an individual could not present their challenge coin during a coin check. In some instances, the individual may even be forced to give up their coin as a result.

So, when the sergeant lifted his coin in the air and slammed it down on the bar top, his fellow officers all followed suit. On this night though, it wasn't just the sergeants party who had served, the bartender that evening had also served in the Coast Guard and didn't have his coin. He'd left it at home.

Unwilling to part with his coin at a later date, the bartender cut a deal with the sergeant. The group would let the bartender off the hook and not demand his challenge coin, but in return, the bartender had to staple one of the Juneau Police Department patches on the wall in a prominent place for all to see.

And for a long time, this was the only patch on the saloon's wall.

However, as the capital city, Juneau plays host to the state troopers as well as a number of police departments from smaller Southeast communities for training. And, on any given night, the saloon would be full of officers from Ketchikan, Sitka, Skagway, or others; and, eventually, those officers got sick and tired of staring at the Juneau PD patch all by itself.

It wasn't long before the state troopers' patch, and other Southeast Alaskan police patches were also up on the wall. And once the door was open to other patches, soon policemen, policewomen, servicemen, and servicewomen from all over the United

States vacationing to Alaska started wanting their patches on the wall.

Today, Juneau has become an international travel destination and, as a result, first responder patches from all over the world are brought here just to be hung on the Red Dog Saloon's wall.

Some are even mailed in!

What is the deal with the life preservers?

When one thinks of the Red Dog Saloon, one generally thinks of red, not orange. But several life rings hang above the saloon's main entrance. The rings come from fishing barges, cruise ships, Coast Guard ships, Navy ships, you name it.

And at least once a summer, one ship captain thinks they deserve to join the club, only they neither realize why nor how one gets their life ring hung on the wall. Thankfully, now they—and you—can find out how to get a life ring swinging on their wall by reading this tale about how the Red Dog got its first preserver.

So, as the story goes, the first life preserver was hung at the saloon during the peak of the Cold War. During this time, tensions were high in Alaska due to its proximity to the USSR. United States Navy and Coast Guard ships constantly filled Juneau's ports, crowding the Gastineau Channel and acting as a constant reminder of the dangers just across the Bering Strait.

With this increased military presence, came a change in patronage in the bars and saloons around town, many of which became popular watering holes for the growing number of servicemen and servicewomen trying to forget about the dangers just outside the doors. The Red Dog was no different.

Day after day, these folks would come into the saloon after their rounds, get a pint or a whiskey, and sit at tables in little clusters, whispering in hushed tones about what could happen. Times were bleak.

And it was during this time that one of the bartenders at the saloon had had enough. He couldn't just keep filling their glasses and hoping for the best. He felt the need to do something, anything, to raise the spirits of those protecting the nation and spark a sense of pride in the townspeople of Juneau.

So, he went down to the docks to hopefully speak to someone in the Navy about hanging one of their flags in the bar to support the men and women serving the country. The bartender explained that he wanted those protecting the nation to know that we stood with them; and that we all stood together against evil. He finished by stating that there was no higher honor than defending the United States against those who sought to cause the nation harm—an effort that deserved to be recognized.

Although the Navy officer was moved by the sentiment, he hesitated to give away one of his flags to hang in the saloon. Thankfully, he wasn't the only one listening to the conversation. A captain of one of the Coast Guard vessels docked in Juneau happened to be walking by at the time and, having heard the bartender's request, he was happy to help how he could.

Later that day, the captain came by the saloon with a life preserver from his ship. He explained that, unfortunately, they couldn't let go of any flags since they were the only things helping other vessels identify the good guys from the bad, but a life ring, well, a life ring they could spare. The bartender took that

Coast Guard ship's life ring without hesitation and put it up on the saloon's wall that very same day as a symbol of gratitude and respect.

Word quickly spread about the gesture and, before long, other ships in port started sending their own life rings to be hung in the bar. Soon, the saloon's walls were covered with bright orange rings, each representing a different unit in the Coast Guard or Navy, and the camaraderie between Alaska's people and those who protect their waters.

The people of Alaska felt a sense of pride and comfort knowing that their local bar supported those who protected their shores. And every time they walked into the Red Dog Saloon, they were reminded of the sacrifices the Coast Guard and Navy were making, and the importance of standing together.

Years passed, and the Cold War ended. Still, the life rings remain, reminding the people of the importance of unity and support during trying times. The tradition of hanging rings continues to this day, only now the saloon welcomes life preservers from any ship that contributes to the prosperity of the city of Juneau and the state of Alaska.

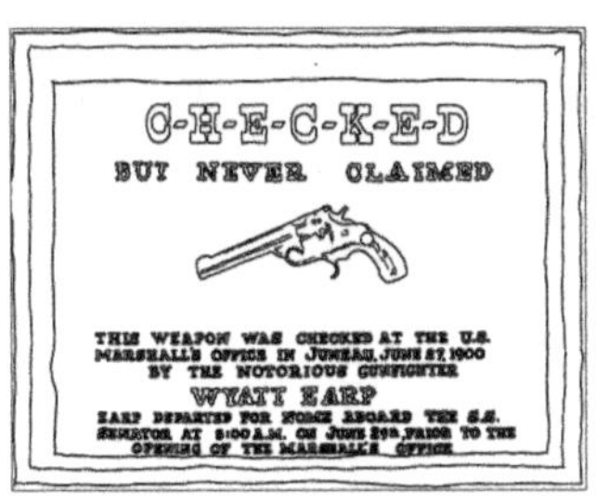

That (Wyatt Earp's) pistol's fake, right?

From what I can tell, most people think the pistol attributed to Wyatt Earp hanging at the Red Dog Saloon is a fake—a silly gimmick to get the cruise ship tourists to come into the saloon and spend money. And no matter how hard I try to tell them, or explain the story, there is no convincing them of its authenticity. Perhaps, after reading it in black and white, now they'll believe me.

All right, so many know the story of

the legendary lawman of the American West, Wyatt Earp—they've heard the stories about Dodge City, or they've read about his famous gunfights in Arizona, but what they don't know is that Wyatt Earp made the long trip up to Alaska in the late nineteenth century.

While the exact reason for his trip remains unclear, there are several theories for why Earp came to Alaska. Some say it was his desire for adventure; others say it was his lawman mentality pushing him to tame the Klondike's lawless environment, but most just believe it was the possibility of striking it rich.

Either way, the Klondike gold rush was a significant event in the late 1800s, attracting thousands of prospectors to the north in search of wealth, and Earp was no different. Earp's travels to Alaska weren't without challenges and setbacks though, and one such setback occurred upon his arrival in Juneau.

Earp's quick trigger reputation and marksmanship had made him a bit of a liability for the local marshal at the time, so he had his deputies meet Wyatt on-board the ferry and make him check his pistol before disembarking. At least, this is how the story goes.

Authorities in Juneau, indeed, would confiscate the firearms of passers-through to prevent outsiders from coming into town, shooting up the place, and then moving on; however, Wyatt was no normal passenger. He was a lawman himself after all, and should have been trusted. But it didn't matter. Earp's past profession wasn't even considered because the authorities confiscated his sidearm at the request of the US Marshal's office in Arizona.

Now, as many of you may remember, Wyatt Earp was involved in a pretty famous gunfight with the Clanton gang at the O.K. Corral in Tombstone, Arizona.

But what you might not know is that this was not where the fighting ended. The remaining members of the Clanton gang sought out Earp after that faithful day in Tombstone and ended up killing Earp's brother, Morgan, as revenge.

Well, Wyatt didn't take too kindly to that, so him and Doc Holiday took justice into their own hands, raiding well-known outlaw hideouts and killing those suspected of being involved in Morgan's murder. These murders, and his actions in Tombstone, had earned Earp a murder indictment in Arizona, giving him one heck of a reason to flee somewhere very far away—Alaska—and a pretty darn good reason for the marshals here in Juneau to try and slow him down.

Having been a marshal himself once upon a time, it didn't take Earp too long to figure out the truth behind being relieved of his pistol. However, when he did, there really wasn't much he could do about it. The ferry system in Alaska back then was sporadic at best, with only one boat coming through Juneau every month or so. This meant that, to continue to avoid the Arizona Marshals, Earp would need to continue on to Nome, Alaska at his scheduled departure time, 5:00 a.m. the next day.

Unfortunately, to collect his pistol, he would need to be in Juneau when the marshal's office opened at 9 a.m. And, because you're reading this story right now, I'm guessing you can probably tell what Wyatt decided to do.

And that explains the how—and why—Wyatt Earp checked in his pistol in Juneau, and never claimed it. What it doesn't tell you though, is how exactly the Red Dog Saloon ended up with it.

And friends, well, that is a different story entirely.

If it (Wyatt Earp's pistol) isn't fake, how did it end up here?

Okay, now that we know how the pistol got to Alaska, the next logical question is, "How did the saloon get it?" And I'm happy to answer you, but to do so, I'll first have to provide you with a little history about Earp's time here in Alaska and what came next.

So, presumably Earp came to Alaska to mine for gold, right? Well, being the intelligent man he was, he quickly realized that it was a lot easier making money selling beer to miners than mining for gold himself. So, Earp opened a bar in Nome, Alaska.

And boy, did he make out like a bandit! Rumor has it, Earp left Nome with roughly $80,000 on him, which is more than $2 million today after adjusting for inflation.

Now, the reason for his departure is just as unknown as his reason for the trip up to Alaska in the first place. Still, one thing is for sure, his time in Alaska did nothing to tarnish his reputation as one of the most legendary figures in American history. And after his passing in Los Angeles, the pistol he left in Juneau became somewhat of a historic piece of memorabilia from the Alaskan gold rush.

At the time, Alaska was still a territory of the United States; therefore, there were fewer rules, governing laws, and loyal officials upholding the rule of law. And it was precisely this wild-west environment that opened the door for shady behavior and for the Red Dog Saloon to gain possession of the pistol.

If you can recall from the previous story, Earp's pistol was temporarily surrendered to the marshals upon arriving in Juneau. And it stayed with them for some time, at least until his death.

When Earp died, the gun was surrendered to the territorial museum here in Juneau for display. This much we know. But as for the exact circumstances surrounding how Earp's gun came to be in the saloon's possession, well, let's just say they aren't as well documented. If you ask any of the locals though, you'll find that this famous deposit was actually made by one of Alaska's first museum curators.

By all accounts, in and around the time of Earp's death, the museum curator here in town was a bit of a lush. And in order to afford his nasty little habit, he would go around town, building up large tabs with the local bartenders and bar owners, and paying those tabs off with memorabilia from the museum. Well, the original Red Dog Saloon bar owner knew about this and decided to use it to his advantage.

The man was a bit of a munitions collector and wanted that pistol badly. So, what did he do? He told his bartenders to let the curator's tab grow just a little larger than anyone else around town would allow. And they did, pouring him top-shelf spirits whenever possible, and filling his friend's cups whenever he asked. That way, when it came time to call in the curator's debt, the only thing in that museum worth anywhere close to what was owed would be Wyatt Earp's pistol.

It has hung behind the bar ever since.

Whose shoes are those?

As you know, and as we've already discussed, Wyatt Earp's pistol hangs behind the bar. But what you might not know or what you might have missed, is a pair of female, old-time leather shoes hung just to the side of the pistol.

Don't worry, many people overlook this little addition to the saloon's decor. But since you're reading this book, I'm guessing you're interested in the history of the saloon. And if that's the case, you really need to pay attention to this story.

Hattie Jessup, the queen of ragtime—or as many called her, the silver dollar lady on account of her lavish silver dollar halter top—was a ragtime pianist and staple at the Red Dog Saloon during the 1950s. She was a fixture at the place, as much a part of the decor as the dark wood paneling on the walls and the flickering gas lamps hanging from the chandeliers. And, on many nights, her music was the soundtrack to the lives of the saloon's loyal patrons.

Her listeners came from all walks of life. The miners would come in with mud on their boots and dust on their clothes, looking for a drink and a little entertainment. The government representatives and downtown business people would stop by on their way home from the office, hoping to unwind and forget about the stresses of their day.

And then there were the ladies, who would slip in through the back door, careful not to be seen by anyone they knew, and dance the night away in their fancy dresses and high heels.

Hattie loved them all, each and every one of them. She loved the way they tapped their feet to her music, sang along to the familiar tunes, laughed, joked, and even flirted with her. She was a part of their lives and a friend to them all.

Unfortunately, after years of playing, her fingers began to fail her and her voice strained when trying to hit the high notes. Not to mention, she was tired of staying up all night, night after night. When this occurred, she decided that it was time for her to retire.

She knew that her regulars would resist and beg her to stay. So, one night, after the last note had been played and the last drink had been poured, Hattie slipped off into the night without saying goodbye to anyone. But as Hattie walked out the door, she felt a pang in her heart and turned to take one last look at the place. She looked at the sawdust on the floor, the animals hanging from the walls, and the red velvet cloth covering her piano; it had all been such a large part of her life. So, instead of simply walking away, Hattie left a little piece of herself for the bar and its patrons.

Hattie slipped off her shoes and left them under the piano. The shoes were worn and scuffed and the leather was cracked and creased from years of use, but in her mind, they were the perfect symbol of what she'd given over the years to the Red Dog and her listeners.

The next day, when the saloon opened its doors, the regulars found Hattie's shoes under the piano. Some were confused, but some laughed, remembering when they'd seen Hattie playing her piano barefoot, toes tapping on the pedals. Others, though, felt a twinge of sadness, realizing Hattie might never return. And as the days passed, they realized this to be true.

Nonetheless, they all took solace in the beat-down leather boots she'd left them, acting as a reminder of all the good times they'd shared. And to mirror their appreciation for Hattie, the saloon hung the boots behind the bar up front and center, reminding everyone to always appreciate what they have before it's gone.

Who is Phineas Poon?

Those who work at and learn to love the Red Dog Saloon often lose a piece of themselves to the place. And when that happens, they tend to leave that little piece of themselves at the bar when they move on. Some leave a signature on the wall, some leave their torn-up leather boots, and some, well, they leave a bit more.

Now, there are more than a few fascinating artifacts in the gun cases behind the bar: pistols, handcuffs, and famous rifles litter the walls. But that's not all that's in there. If you look closer, you'll also see some special bottles.

There are dusty whiskey bottles adorning their original 1866 labeling; there are bottles of whiskey that have a label on them specifically for the Red Dog Saloon; and there's even a bottle filled with human remains on the top shelf!

That's right, Phineas Poon, or as his friends knew him, Tag, has his final resting place on the highest shelf behind the bar. But before we understand the why and how, let's first look into the who.

Tag was a longtime entertainer and piano player at the Red Dog Saloon. He came to the bar in the summer of 1971, claiming the spell of Alaska was something he just couldn't ignore. During his time, he saw the saloon change locations and ownership, and he bore witness to the city of Juneau change from a mining town to a tourist town.

This was perfectly A-Okay with Tag because he loved the tourists, or as he called them, boat people. And the boat people loved him back. He had this magical way about him, a way that allowed him to single anyone out of the crowd, make fun of where they were from, talk badly about what they were wearing, and even shoot them with a water gun without consequence.

It was this magic that made the Red Dog Saloon an essential stop in Juneau and had people coming from all over the world to see him. But his jokes, and entertaining spirit, transcended the stage as well, making him a favorite among the locals and his colleagues behind the bar. One of his favorite jokes was that he was never going to leave the saloon. He'd say, "Just shove my ashes on the top shelf, I'm going to haunt this place forever anyway."

Everyone laughed at this joke, that is, until the winter that Tag fell ill and passed away suddenly. It was terrible. The community had not only lost an incredible entertainer, but they'd also lost a friend.

But before Tag passed, to ensure his wishes were honored, he'd commissioned a special whiskey bottle with his face and a few of his witty remarks on the label, and presented it to the owner of the saloon. Upon doing so, he told the owner there was no place he'd rather be, and asked to be placed somewhere special. And that's exactly where he's been ever since, a permanent fixture on the highest shelf behind the bar.

Over the years, the bottle has become part of Tag's legacy, allowing his memory and humor to live on in the little Alaskan saloon. But not everyone is excited about Tag's ashes in the saloon. Some claim he still wanders the bar at night, playing pranks on the closing bartenders and servers. Either way, though, if you do see a shadow out of the corner of your eye, or witness an unexplained spinning chandelier, you just need to remember that if its Tag, it is all in good fun.

Is there anything else interesting in the gun cases?

As you've already learned from the previous stories, the Red Dog Saloon in Juneau, Alaska, is a legendary establishment that has existed since the late 1800s. You've also learned about bits and pieces of the eclectic memorabilia on our walls, including famous firearms. Of course, Wyatt Earp's pistol, which you read about earlier, is the collection's crown jewel, but some of the others are also incredibly rare and valuable.

From what I know, one of the weapons hanging in the left case, which has been beautifully preserved and looks like it could still be fired today, is from World War I. Right underneath that rests a rifle from World War II, a fascinating piece of history that has seen its fair share of action. And, if you prefer Americana, kitty-corner to the world war weapons hangs a musket loader from the Civil War.

But perhaps the most intriguing item in the collection is a rifle made famous by the Hollywood movie, "The Birdman of Alcatraz." It is said that the double-barrel shotgun in the top right corner of the case to the right was used by the now famous Birdman himself.

For those who don't know, the Birdman lived in Juneau for some time before he went to prison. And from what I've been told, he was known as a bit of an oddball. Still, nobody suspected he could commit the terrible act that would eventually make him, and the saloon's double-barrel shotgun, famous.

According to the rumors, the Birdman's wife used to work at the bar where the Red Dog Saloon now stands, Sweeny's. And at this same time, a handsome and charming Russian bartender also worked there. The two took to each other quickly, and it wasn't long before they ended up in bed together. The affair continued for some time without anyone knowing. But eventually, the Birdman caught wind of what was going on. And, having become consumed with jealousy and rage, he hatched a plan to confront the two lovebirds.

So, one evening, when his wife was "closing the bar," he decided to follow her to Sweeny's and wait. When he saw the two leaving the bar together, the Birdman followed them to the bartender's house and with the very shotgun we're talking about, shot them both in cold blood.

The shocking crime left the community reeling and sent the Birdman to a federal penitentiary for twelve years. And he would have gotten out, had it not been for the Birdman's terrible temper. While incarcerated, he stabbed and killed a guard, stamping his one-way ticket to a life sentence in Alcatraz.

Despite his terrible crime, the Birdman has become a legend in his own right because of the movie. A classic film about a man training the birds that flew into his cell, and the power of redemption and the resilience of the human spirit.

On the other hand, his shotgun still hanging at the Red Dog Saloon tells a different story, one that serves as a chilling reminder of the darker side of human nature and the fragility of human life.

Author's Note

As you come to the end of this book of tall tales, we hope you have enjoyed the wild adventures and colorful characters that have been brought to life through the stories of Alaska's gold rush and the world-famous Red Dog Saloon in Juneau.

But it is important to remember that, although these tales have been shared and passed down by locals over the years, they are not entirely factual. They are the stuff of legend and imagination, embellished with each retelling to become bigger and more outrageous than before.

Nonetheless, these stories have become an integral part of the fabric of Alaska's history and culture, and they continue to inspire and entertain new generations of storytellers and listeners.

So, as you put down this book, remember to take these tales with a grain of salt, and to appreciate them for what they are: a testament to the enduring spirit of the Last Frontier, and to the power of a good story to captivate and delight us all.

Who's your author?

The author telling these tall tales was born and raised in Canada, but he'll tell you he's from Alaska. He'll tell you that because he's spent the last seven years of his life living in Juneau. But it wasn't the picturesque landscapes that brought him here though. No. Instead, it was an unexpected encounter in the heart of South America that made his life take this remarkable turn.

That's right, he followed a woman all the way up north, past the sixtieth parallel. However, their initial meeting was bittersweet. Their whirlwind romance in South America only lasted three weeks because she had a job to get back to in Alaska and, at the time, he had a company to run back in Canada. So, they said farewell and went their separate ways.

But, upon getting home, our author knew that something was different. Something about that girl had left an undeniable mark on his heart. And, driven by this unshakable feeling, he planned a trip to visit her in Juneau.

From the moment he landed in Alaska, he was struck by the towering mountains, lush forests, and the pristine waters reflecting the azure sky above. But, if you ask him now, it was the simple moments spent with the woman he loved that left the deepest impression. Whether it was sharing stories over a crackling fire or embarking on an impromptu hike up Blueberry Hill, every moment felt like a cherished memory.

And with each passing moment they spent together, the author's resolve to build a future with her grew stronger. So, with unwavering determination, he returned home to Canada, knowing that his heart was still in Alaska. He sold his shares in the company and everything else he owned, and embarked on the greatest adventure of his life.

Seven years later, he's now married to the woman he met in South America, and a proud resident of Juneau, Alaska. A place that has not only become his home, but the backdrop to his very own love story—the greatest story he'll ever tell.

www.ingramcontent.com/pod-product-compliance
Lightning Source LLC
Chambersburg PA
CBHW040212170726
48295CB00013B/642
* 9 7 8 1 9 5 4 8 9 6 3 8 3 *